AIRLOCK

AIRLOCK

Tash McAdam

orca soundings

ORCA BOOK PUBLISHERS

Published in Canada and the United States in 2023 by Orca Book Publishers.
orcabook.com

Library and Archives Canada Cataloguing in Publication
Title: Airlock / Tash McAdam.
Names: McAdam, Tash, author.
Series: Orca soundings.
Description: Series statement: Orca soundings
Identifiers: Canadiana (print) 2022045339X | Canadiana (ebook) 2022045342X |
ISBN 9781459836600 (softcover) | ISBN 9781459836617 (PDF) |
ISBN 9781459836624 (EPUB)
Subjects: LCGFT: Thrillers (Fiction) | LCGFT: Action and adventure fiction.
Classification: LCC PS8625.A5582 A75 2023 | DDC jC813/.6—dc23

Library of Congress Control Number: 2022948360

Summary: In this high-interest accessible novel for teen readers,
nonbinary teen Brick must rescue the crew of the spaceship
they snuck onto when it is taken over by pirates.

Orca Book Publishers is committed to reducing the consumption
of nonrenewable resources in the production of our books. We make
every effort to use materials that support a sustainable future.

Orca Book Publishers gratefully acknowledges the support for its publishing
programs provided by the following agencies: the Governmentof Canada,
the Canada Council for the Arts and the Province of British Columbia
through the BC Arts Council and the Book Publishing Tax Credit.

Design by Ella Collier
Edited by Doeun Rivendell
Cover photography by Getty Images/Klaus Vedfelt

Printed and bound in Canada.

26 25 24 23 • 1 2 3 4

To all the librarians out there doing the good work in these hard times. You're saving lives, growing minds and changing hearts.

Chapter One

It's bitter hot inside my hidey-hole. Hot, stinky and dusty. My stolen filter can't keep up, and my chest is tight from struggling to breathe. My eyes are red and sore. Squinting, I look into my small mirror to check over my appearance one more time.

I blink as I take in my reflection. Today I have to be invisible. Just a runner delivering a message to a ship. Nothing like what I *am* going to be. A stowaway.

Making my face go soft, I widen my eyes. The tiny shifts of muscle change me completely. I've had the knack since I was a kid. I used to follow the local trash sorters and mimic their slumped shoulders and dragging feet. People thought that was odd. They think I'm weird. One of the many reasons I don't have a crew or even a friend...if you don't count the mice.

I glance at the corner where I scattered some crumbs of food. The last scraps of my last protein bar. I licked the wrapper clean, but I always save something for my little furry friends. Right now they're nowhere in sight. I haven't seen them since the dust storm two days ago. I hope they won't miss me too much. I hope they don't get caught and thrown into a soup pot without me.

Pulling my attention back to the mirror reassures me I've got the right look. I'm nonbinary, not a boy or a girl, but I can do a good impression of either.

If I have the right clothes and time to style myself, no one ever notices.

Today I've made myself more like a boy. My thick black hair is greasy and messy. My face is soft and innocent. My plump cheeks make me look younger, which will help today. The real me is almost invisible. But my mom's round brown eyes look back at me, just like always. Reminding me who I am. Telling me there's more waiting for me in the universe than this shit heap called Earth.

I'm getting off this barren planet. I didn't plan to do it today, but the arrest warrant with my name on it is forcing me to run. I've thought about leaving often enough that I at least have a plan. If I'm brave enough to pull it off. I shiver, trying not to think of the great, pressing silence of space. At least once a week, I wake up gasping from nightmares about dying inside that black vacuum.

I pull my mask over my mouth and nose, then

flip my collar up. Now I'm just fringe, eyes and a black mask. Satisfied my disguise is perfect, I slip out the back window. The soft rags on my feet don't give good grip, but I'm used to it.

I scramble up the crumbled concrete until I'm standing on what's left of the roof. From here I can see quite a bit of the ruined city. The roads look like someone kicked over an anthill. There are black-clad soldiers crawling everywhere. The Boots, who protect the interests of the rich who've already left this forsaken planet. Who keep taking the last scraps of resources we have on Earth, leaving nothing behind but broken backs and hearts.

Barely visible through the thick red smog that always fills the air, the sun hangs. A promise that there's more out there than this.

My hideout is at the top of an old apartment building that most people are too scared to climb. I don't have neighbors, but enough people know I'm up here that someone will sell me out. If there's a chance at food or fresh, clean water? Most people would sell their own mother for a protein bar. No, I can't hide away. I have to run. Now.

I take a deep breath, my mask pressing tight against my mouth. It's wet with my spit and sweat already.

"You! Stop!" The loud yell draws my attention back down. One street over, a soldier drags a woman out into the street. They're holding her by the hair. While I watch, another soldier pulls a teenager and presses their hand to a tablet to check their identity. I know that teen isn't who they're after.

They're after me.

I woke up this morning to a red alert with my handprint attached. The thick scar slicing across all four of my fingers is a pretty obvious clue. Five years ago a knife would have taken my eye if I hadn't gotten my hand in the way. I thought it was a small price to pay, but now they have enough to find me.

I know exactly how they got my handprint. Five days ago I was helping myself to some supplies that had been left in a "secure" building. I got a little too greedy and tried to take too much. As I left, weighed down by full bags, I tripped! I dropped to one knee and caught myself on my hand. I should have wiped the handprint away. But I didn't think they would check the floor tiles. I got cocky and now I'm paying for it. I have no choice but to get off the planet.

I'd assumed I'd have at least twenty-four hours after the alert, before they figured out where in town to start looking for me. Instead I'll have to get around this violent search party.

The soldiers release the woman and teen and move to the next shack. I shiver and roll across the roof, staying low. Once I'm on the other side, I grab my go bag and run for my escape route. It's a carefully planned climb down the side of the building. A series of almost invisible handholds and toe grips. I'm small and light but also wiry and strong. The tiny muscles on the backs of my brown hands flex as I shift my weight. Careful and fast, I stay in the shadow of the most broken wall all the way to the ground.

Not even stopping to shake out my sore fingers, I slip around a corner onto the biggest street that passes through the town. The local bookie is running a fight in the open, on the broken asphalt of the road. It's a good spot for it, which is one of the reasons I live around here. With the small market in the mornings and the fights in the afternoons, there's usually a crowd. It's easyto get lost in a crowd. There's a good one right now. A horde of people, pushing and shoving a little. In front of them, two women are beating each other to a pulp.

Sprinting past, I yell, "Scatter!"

Chapter Two

Everyone reacts immediately, and I'm caught up in the crowd as I'd hoped.

The best way to stay out of sight is to blend in. A woman with two toddlers is fighting to keep hold of them. A hundred people are trying to get out of the main street. The buildings are all emptying out as the panic catches. No one wants to be caught and sent to the mines or beaten to death.

I grab one of the toddlers and swing the kid up in one arm. Then I wrap my other arm around the woman's waist. She clings on, and I work us out of the crowd.

Soldiers are closing in on the scene, but their eyes pass over me. I'm struggling to carry the toddler and hold on to "my mom." I probably look about twelve. Good. I play it up, eyes wide and tears pumping. Body language screaming young and scared. Much too young to be breaking and entering. Definitely not brave or old enough to be the person they're after.

We break away from the group and turn onto a side street, breathing hard. The Boots will be here any minute. I plop the kid down on a rock.

"Thanks!" I yell as I begin to run. To avoid the Boots, I make a huge loop around the edge of the town. It takes over three hours of walking and jogging. But I finally reach the towering electric fence that surrounds the spaceport.

The port is where spaceships blast off and set down. They deliver criminals here to serve out sentences in the dust. Then they leave again, taking away what's left of Earth's guts. Across the fence I can see mountains of shipping containers, piled high enough to block out the sun. Full of metals and parts for electronics and machines. All harvested from the dying body of our home planet. I pull a disgusted face at the world.

There's a secret entrance through an abandoned house near the back of the spaceport facilities. I creep along the fence, then move into deeper shadow. It's a huge relief.

I lean against a wall for a moment, dripping with sweat. My whole body is tight from nerves and exhaustion. My head is pounding. It feels like there are thorns digging into my temples, winding tighter and tighter. My mouth is sticky and gummy. I can feel bits of dry skin peeling off my lips against my mask. I'm so thirsty, but the small bottle of water in my bag might be all I have.

I fumble for the zipper. I can barely think, so I have to drink. Before I can open my backpack, my neck prickles. I freeze. What's different? I cast my eyes around the shadowy alley.

In the darkness a large shape moves. My heart jumps into my throat as I prepare to run. But before my brain has sent the message to my feet, the shape comes closer. It becomes the large form of Amar. Local enforcer, bouncer and all-around tough. He towers over me, and I shrink away.

My nerves are shot, and I don't know what to expect. I watch him, scared, still catching my breath. "Amar," I say. My voice shakes a bit. I wish I hadn't said anything. I sound like a scared wimp.

"Brick." He says my name like he's dropping a rock. Then he hands over a bottle of cloudy water. I take it gratefully, draining the whole thing in moments. It's rude of me, but I don't care much right now. I probably should. Amar isn't someone to mess with.

If I could pull it off—which I can't, because I'm too short and too small—I would channel Amar when I wanted to scare someone. I'd copy his stone-cold calm, never showing any emotion. When he fights, he doesn't even look angry. He almost looks bored. He has low, heavy eyebrows and a pinched-in mouth. He stands with his shoulders back and his large chin out. His arms are always flexing. My muscles are sneaky. Most people don't notice them. Amar's muscles are *not* sneaky. They are attention-seeking drama kings.

My back is pressed right against the wall. I'm ready to duck, to run. I might still get away. Every moment I spend here is another moment for someone to point the soldiers after me. For them to march down the streets in lockstep, boots thumping.

Every riot that starts ends to the sound of those boots.

Amar is strong, and he's fast at close range, but I bet I can beat him in a sprint. My eyes flick around, looking for a way out. But I can't get past him.

"What's up?" I ask nervously.

"Thought you might be the one they was after."

Chapter Three

Oh no. Is Amar going to turn me over to the Boots? I'm shaking now. My lip trembles with every breath. My shirt is sticking to me, and I can feel a drip of sweat on the end of my nose. It tickles.

"Thought you might be on your way off planet," Amar says.

"That's my plan."

"I want to come?" he says, looking down at his feet.

What?

Amar is the same age as me. Sixteen. Where I can pass for twelve, Amar is truly man-size, in every possible way. He could hold his arm out straight and put his palm on my head. If he pushed down, I'd end up on my knees.

But suddenly he doesn't look like a man anymore. He looks like a scared kid. His whole face has changed. He looks soft and afraid.

"Please. I hate it here," he says.

Does Amar have any family? Does he have anyone? I've never even thought about it. He collects money for the local bosses. And he fights for even more. I'd assumed he liked it.

Damn. "Do you even fit through the Rat Door?" I ask. I hope he says no. He can't blame me for not being able to figure out another way to smuggle him in. As far as I know, there are only two ways in and out of the port. The front door and the Rat Door. The front door isn't an option.

"I can get small." The puppy-dog eyes Amar makes are record-breaking. I already know what I'm going to say. I've always been soft.

I jerk my chin in agreement and start walking. My heart thumps at the thought that I might've forgotten the way. That I won't even find the right place. All these abandoned houses—too close to the port to be livable, with the noise and pollution—look kind of the same. Broken down and slumping. The Rat House one of them.

But once I get inside, I'll know I've got it. There! I spot a crack I recognize and duck through the empty entrance.

That's it. There's the door. Gulp.

I've been through it only once before. But it was on my way *out* of the port, after being stuck inside for twenty-one days. I'd made a bad mistake and picked the wrong shipment to rob. I got stuck, and the truck took me all the way into the port. I was trapped there, hiding in the middle of the load.

Once it got dark, I'd tried to find a way out, but I couldn't. There wasn't one. I lived off garbage and stolen water, waiting to get caught. The smart thing to do would have been to get off the planet then. But I was too afraid. I worked myself up to it again and again. But every time the moment came, I'd freeze. My feet wouldn't move, and I'd miss the chance. Then, a few days later, there'd be another moment. Just one second where I could get onto a transport ship if I just went for it.

The trip to the moon is short. Everything goes to the massive station around the moon before being shipped out farther. From there I would've had my pick of space stations to escape to. I might have been able to steal some ID and become a real person.

I could have gone. But I was too scared.

So I'd stayed, day after day. Chance after chance flew away into the sky. Then I saw the smuggler. The moment I noticed the guy, I knew he wasn't legit. The way he walked gave it away. A man with a sneaky, uncomfortable air. When I heard the way he swore, I was sure. He was as out of place there as I was. I followed him out through the Rat Door, and he never even noticed.

Now I don't have a choice. It isn't safe on Earth anymore.

I have to find the secret way to open the door.

I run my hands across the pocked surface carefully. The metal scrapes against my sensitive fingers. I have a few blood blisters from my fast climb. But I keep going until I find something. There's a groove in the metal. When I hook my fingers into it, I feel a hidden dent. It pulls like a handle. The door groans as it opens, dust moving out of cracks as the sheet of metal shifts. It reveals a dark tunnel.

Behind me, Amar is breathing hard. I feel his huge hand on my shoulder. I freeze in response. Are the soldiers here? Is he about to hand me over? But he just rubs his thumb on my shoulder blade. I've tensed up, I realize. Every muscle in my back is knotted under his hand.

The tunnel is steep. Underfoot, small pebbles move. I try to pretend I'm not scared of the dark. But after the door closes, it's pitch-black. As black as space, an endless, empty void. The ceiling is brushing my hair, and I'm almost grateful for it. I'm five foot five on my tallest day. Amar must be bent in half. Even though it's not comfortable, the solid surfaces around us remind me I'm not about to drift away into the night. I brush my shoulder against the rough stones. They pull at the ragged fabric of my sleeve. *I'm on solid ground. It's dark but not dangerous,* I tell myself. I'm not very convincing.

We creep downward, under the electric fence

that guards the port. The tunnel is so hot my lungs hurt. Amar keeps his hand on my shoulder. He stays so close behind me I can feel his breath on my neck. I don't mind. Usually I would. I've never been much for people. After my mom died, I stuck to myself as much as possible. Too many messed-up people out there. But I find myself leaning back into Amar's hand, just a bit.

The darkness is so deep I can't tell if my eyes are open or closed. If it wasn't for Amar behind me, I'm not sure I'd still be walking. I wish I'd brought a torch or a candle. I wish I *had* a torch or a candle to bring. If I had a lighter, I think I'd set fire to my sleeve just for a moment of sight. My imagination is playing tricks on me. There must be enough air. My chest feels tight. I'm gasping, but there's no oxygen.

Chapter Four

"Brick! Brick!" Amar shakes me, and air rushes back into my lungs. There are bright spots dancing in my eyes. It seems unfair that they don't light up the tunnel.

Slowly my panic fades out. I take deep breaths, counting inside my head. Then I start shuffling forward again.

There's no way to see, so I trip when the floor levels out. I expected it to keep going down. I bite my lip, trying not to shout in pain as my knee bashes into the ground.

Strong hands help me up—Amar's. He dusts me off as best he can in the small space and then pushes me forward. He's gentle, but I have to keep going. The ground starts to tilt up. We're going back to the surface.

The tunnel ends all of a sudden. I would have fallen again if Amar hadn't caught me. I'm not usually clumsy, but the dark is throwing me off. The walls of packed dirt and stones feel like they're closing in. There's a tickle in my throat, and I know if I cough it will be loud. Loud enough to be heard outside?

My heart is thundering—or is it soldiers' boots? The space is too small! I can't turn around.

Amar takes my hand and holds it for a long minute. Then he squeezes it and places it on a metal bar. It's cold against my hot palm. It calms me. I take a deep breath again. I'd probably still be stuck at the bottom of the tunnel if it wasn't for Amar. I can't believe I thought I could do this alone. If the tunnel almost did me in, how will I manage in the *real* crushing dark of space?

"Thanks," I say, before climbing the ladder attached to the wall. It goes up into a circular opening and into a vertical tunnel. At the top, my head thuds against something, the sound echoing. It's worse than if I'd coughed. My ears ring, but I can't tell if it's inside my head or outside. It was a metal cover over the exit. I knew it was going to be there, but it surprised me anyway.

Nothing to be done about it now. I move more carefully this time. Feeling around with my fingertips reveals nothing. No lock or catch. I press my shoulder into the metal and heave. It's heavy, but I manage to shove it out of the way, a few inches at a time. I don't waste more time worrying about being noisy. Either we get caught or we don't. On we go.

Amar follows me out and looks around. He's probably never been inside the port before, but there's nothing much to see right now. We're inside a shipping container. It's not as dark as the tunnel, thanks to holes drilled in the roof. Spears of light come in at an angle, letting us see the dusty space. It looks exactly like any other empty container, except that this one is part of a smugglers' path.

When I look back at Amar, he's grinning. I'm not sure I've ever seen him smile before. It's nice, and I grin back. It's sort of okay to have someone with me. For as long as I can remember, I've been afraid of suffocating in an airless space. The first time I took the tunnel, I had a light. Even then I almost didn't make it through. At times I thought I'd sit on the floor, gasping for breath and unable to move, until a smuggler found me. It was easier this time, with Amar behind me. Maybe the rest will be better too.

Inside the container, everything is muffled. There are distant roars, clangs and bangs. They're the normal sounds of a working port, but every noise makes me twitch. Magnetic shuttles pass up and down at all hours along the suspension cables. On the far side of the port are the spaceships. When I was younger, I used to come and watch them. I'd watch all night sometimes. Counting the bright moving points of light in the sky. Waiting for one to get bigger, bigger, until the whole world rattled with sound. Until everything was noise and fury and I couldn't hear my own thoughts.

I'm trying very hard not to think about going into space. I'm also ignoring the part of my brain trying to list all the ways I could die today or tomorrow. Getting caught leads to death. The slow way, chained up in a mining crew. Or the fast way, shot by some soldier who finds me on board.

But there's no choice now. My life of stealing and starving here is done.

Amar is waiting for me to do something. I can tell by the way he's watching me. I'm in charge here—I'm the one with a plan. Or a hope and a dream, at least.

In the corner of the container there's a crate. I tiptoe across the metal floor, careful not to make any more sound. I've no idea how loud a noise inside here would be. I don't want to find out! The crate is made of light-gray plastic with a huge clip securing it. My sweaty, trembling fingers slip on the plastic as I fiddle with the clip. But I manage to grip and squeeze the sides. It takes every ounce of my finger strength to pop the clip open.

The crate lid releases. There's a gap an inch wide. I pause. When I open the crate, I'll find out if my plan is possible. Do I want to know? I try to swallow, but it feels like there's a piece of glass in my throat.

A big hand reaches past me. Amar has thin black hairs on the backs of his hands. Mine are almost bald. His hairs look soft. Amar doesn't notice me looking. He just heaves open the heavy crate lid.

Inside the crate are the same type of bags I saw last time I was here. I exhale in relief, then grab one and unroll the top to check. Yes! Two full water canteens, rations, a small first-aid kit and a pair of earplugs.

Excited, I clench my fist and grin. Amar taps his fist against mine, smiling back. We press our shoulders together for a moment. His is strong and soft at the same time. Somehow it doesn't make me feel small.

We grab two bags each. They belong to the smugglers, who will probably be very upset. They might even care enough to track us down in the future. I can't worry about that now though. This is the only way I can think of to get supplies for the journey. There's not enough water in the slums to store for later. Same with food. I'm always hungry, and putting away even a little would have been awful.

I'm a thief anyway. My whole thing is taking what I need. So what if these guys are scarier than the average merchant?

Amar pushes my shoulder gently, and I realize I've stopped moving. I was frozen in thought, a bad habit of mine when I'm scared.

Reminding myself that the only way off this planet is to *go off this planet*, I steel myself.

Chapter Five

We walk to the other end of the container, where a metal bar runs from top to bottom. It's mirrored by one on the outside. They work in unison so the door can be opened from either side. There's a hole to look out. I peer through it. Nothing but metal containers as far as the eye can see. But all it would take is one person coming around the corner. One drone flying overhead.

Biting the inside of my cheeks, I wrap both hands around the bar and brace myself.

Amar stays close behind me like a shadow. The bar moves easily, and the door opens. It's well oiled and clean. I hope the smugglers don't have a camera on the entrance. I hope they don't have one in here. They probably do. If so, I hope they're not watching it now. All I am is a stack of hopes. Everything about this plan relies on us being lucky.

Just before I slip through the open door, I whisper to Amar, "Keep your head down. Follow my feet." I hope he understands. If there are drones or cameras, someone might come looking. Military or smugglers, one or the other. They'll both want blood. Footage of the tops of our heads will be harder to analyze.

I don't run, because running draws attention. My plan to slip through as a messenger is long gone. The soldiers' search for me in town has pulled security off the port though. That's good for us. It's pretty quiet, but I listen hard for any noise. I have

good ears, able to pick out the whine of drones...
even through the heavy chug of the huge magnetic
shipments inching up the cables. The occasional
shouted order rings off metal walls. Whenever I
hear anything, I turn us away from it. We weave
through the maze of large metal boxes. It's like a
giant has piled them up, a city of stacked iron.

We're in the shadows, making our way around.
We ease through spaces not meant for people. The
gaps where cranes can seize the containers are
barely two feet wide. I have no idea how Amar is
contorting himself to follow me, and I don't have
space to turn and look. We inch forward, pressed
on every side. My mouth is so dry. I wish I'd taken a
drink in the safety of the container. Too late now. We
have to get on a ship. Preferably one that's leaving
soon.

When we reach the edge of the shipyard, I stop.
It's brightly lit. Amar leans against me. He's so tall,
my head is against his chest. His heart is beating fast.

It reminds me of the mice I've held in my hands. Some people ate them, but I never could. They were so small and soft and scared. They were my friends. I wonder if Amar is my friend. He's chosen to leave with me, but I don't know if he'll want to stay together after the trip. Moons, we might not even survive the trip! And now I want to know.

"Do you have a plan?" I ask, quiet as one of my mice. "After."

He looks at me, his big black eyes dark and serious. Like storm clouds. I can almost hear the thunder of his heart. "No. I just can't stay here," he says.

"Same, bro," I say, nodding. "You want to stick together?"

He nods so quickly that I smile.

"Yeah," he says. "Yes, please."

No one says please! He's so polite. There's a warm little ball of good feeling in my chest. "Great," I say to my new friend. "Let's go get on a ship."

There are two cargo ships close enough that they might work. The closest squats like a frog. Its doors are sealed, even the crew hatch. I squint across the bright, dusty grounds. It looks pretty new. Might even have one of those fancy AIs that track all the ship's systems and passengers. Can't fool a robot.

The other ship looks older. But there's no way we'll make it across the open ground without being seen. Amar is big enough to look like a man. His outfit is shapeless and thick with dust, like everyone else's. At a glance, it might seem like he works here. There are two men dressed like him loading the older cargo ship. It's massive, and it has two shuttles, which is unusual. The back door is open, yawning like a great mouth. The metal walkway comes out like a tongue. The men push carts up it and unload large crates. Very large crates.

Amar doesn't ask questions, which I like. I don't mind explaining things if there's time, but right now there isn't. He's happy to follow my lead, which makes things easier. We work our way to the far side of the loading bay. My heart pounds so loudly I'm sure a drone will pick us up.

The two men have about fifteen more crates of different sizes to load, but I can tell they're exhausted. Sure enough, after loading one more crate, they stop to rest in the shade.

If I can pull this off, if Amar can trust me and move fast, we might just manage this after all. I grab Amar's hand and wait for the perfect moment. His fingers are thick and strong, twitching against my palm. There! The men get distracted looking at something on a tablet, and I bolt.

Amar runs with me, quiet despite his size. Puffs of dust burst under our feet. A glance at the workers makes my heart seize. The men are about to get up. Yanking Amar behind me, I use one last spurt of energy to sprint up the walkway. Metal clangs, but I don't look. Can't look.

Into the belly of the ship we run, my heart in my throat. There could be someone checking off supplies in here. But this is our only chance. We don't have time to wait for the perfect opportunity.

Chapter Six

Inside the ship, I dart to one side, pressing against the metal wall. Amar crouches next to me. We are both panting for breath, scanning the room. The grubby cargo bay is stacked high with all sorts of crates on pallets. Everything is old and battered, except for one section. A small chunk of the space is filled by bright-white cubes. I've never seen this type of box before. They look expensive. They're made of some kind of smooth, gleaming material. Instead of sharp corners they have curves. I can't see how they open. My fingers twitch with the urge to check them out. To see if there's anything worth stealing inside. Maybe later.

A further scan of the bay shows massive metal brackets providing the main structure for the ship. Like giant ribs. They stick out almost three feet from the wall, and between each is a six-foot gap. I haul Amar around a neat stack of crates and into one of these nooks. It's easily the best hiding spot I can see at a glance. Concealed between two metal ribs, and with the shelter of the crates in front, we should be invisible.

I hope.

My breathing is fast and choppy, my chest heaving. I've worked hard today, and I'm exhausted.

Amar jumps when I sit down. By *sit down*, I mean my legs went wobbly and I half fell to the floor. Through my thin shirt and trousers, I can feel cold steel pressing against me. Soon that's the only thing that will be between us and the endless, empty expanse of space. I push my forehead into the hard bones of my knees and try to breathe.

In, out. In, out. There will be no air soon, just space.

Amar drops down next to me with a thump. His big body squeezes against my side, and I don't resist when he pulls me against him. I'm soft, like putty.

"My dad used to get panic attacks," Amar says. His voice is smooth and calm. I'm so cold. I lean into him, his warm strength. "That's right. Just breathe. You is okay." He rubs a slow circle on my back, and I breathe with it.

I don't know when I fall asleep. The stress and drama of the day catch up with me at once. I'm blinking slow and heavy, listening to scraps of Amar's soft voice. The next thing I know, I'm jolted awake.

The whole world is shaking, thundering. It's the loudest thing I've ever heard. The ship is taking off!

I'm so stupid! I reach for the supply bags and fiddle with the straps. The small packs of earplugs slip out of my sweaty fingers. It takes me two tries. The engine noise is so loud I cover one ear with my shoulder, desperately grabbing for the soft silicone plugs.

Got them!

It's hard to turn in our small den, our knees and elbows all banging. Not that anyone would hear over the sounds of the furious engine.

I crouch over Amar, who has both hands pressed to his ears. His eyes are scrunched shut, and his face is twisted in pain. My bones rattle with the ship. With clumsy fingers I shove Amar's right hand aside and push the plug in. I drop the second earplug on his thigh and fumble my own plugs out of their packet.

The noise drops off as soon as I shove them in. The takeoff is still shaking every part of me, but I can think. The relief is so intense, I tear up. Amar has his second plug in now and is looking at me.

His eyes are wide and afraid. I can't comfort him because I'm terrified too.

This is it. We're going into space.

We can't talk. We can't sleep—it's like being inside a toy a toddler is shaking. Miserable and uncomfortable, we brace ourselves as best we can. The awful ride goes on forever, and then it stops. Everything goes quiet. For a moment I think I've gone deaf, except for the ringing in my ears. Then I remember the earplugs. I take them out, and sound comes back.

Amar copies me, then puts his plugs back into their case with careful hands. We must have burst out of Earth's atmosphere. And into the deep dark. I wonder how long before we arrive at the moon. I open my mouth to ask Amar what he thinks and then snap it closed. There could be crew checking that cargo didn't shift during takeoff. There could be someone coming into the bay right now. I strain my ears, listening, but my hearing is shot. The muffled ringing has settled into a pinching headache.

I send up a silent prayer of thanks to anything that might listen. Thanks for the supplies, and the friend, and the ship. My luck has been almost unbelievably good.

As soon as I think it, I hear footsteps. It's as though I've summoned bad luck. I flap my hand wildly at Amar, and he stares at me, eyes wide and round. I press myself away from the small "entrance," hoping no one comes to this side of the bay.

Two shadows fall across the floor of the cargo hold, but they're not moving. They seem to be standing by the fascinating white boxes. I thrum with nerves.

"Here they are, Captain." The voice is deep and loud.

"Ten thousand queens. And all of them able to start their own colony. Incredible." The captain's voice is softer, awed. It reminds me of my mother in a way that makes my shoulders roll in.

"You're not so bad yourself." Deep Voice laughs.

I hear a soft thump and a faint whoosh of air, then more laughing. "Put me down, underling!" the captain squawks through laughter. It's hard to stay afraid when they're being so silly. I've never heard of anyone government being silly. Laughing, sure. But in a "Ha ha, I tripped you and now you've spilled your water rations" kind of way. Not in a fun way.

"What'll ya give me?" Deep Voiced Silly Man has moved enough that I can see him. He's a large Black man with a shaved head. His brown jumpsuit is around his waist. Underneath it he's wearing some bright orange-and-red fabric that gleams in the lights. He's got the captain slung over his shoulders. She's plump and brown-skinned. Her dark hair is plaited tightly away from her face.

"A promotion! You can be captain!" The woman giggles, and I realize he's tickling her. This large man, on a spaceship, is *tickling* his captain.

My brain does a sort of stutter stop. *What?* I wonder if they're on some kind of mood enhancers.

Thankfully, this confusing interaction seems to be ending.

"You'll never make me captain! Never!" the man shrieks as he thunders up the metal stairs. "All this lousy crew does is…" I don't get to find out what the lousy crew does, because his voice fades away into the distance.

Amar looks tired and afraid, hunched in on himself. He's pushed against a metal rib, curled up with his knees against his chest. I give him a weak smile, and he returns it. Now that it's quiet, exhaustion weighs heavy on me like a blanket. Amar blinks slowly, and I yawn. I'm too tired to think.

We fall asleep in a pile, using each other for warmth.

The next hours pass in a haze of napping and waking. From time to time one of our limbs slips, and we're jarred awake. We take sips of water and small bites of food when our stomachs growl. We stretch as best we can in the small space and wait. And wait.

And wait.

Chapter Seven

Time passes. There's no way to tell how much. I'm sure the trip to the moon is less than half a day. At night I've watched ships their entire way up.

After a while sleep leaves me alone. At every slight movement the ship makes, I think this is it, the landing. Getting off without being caught could be even harder than getting on board. My mind races through imagined scenes of unloading. I have no idea how it will go, so it's useless thinking about it. But I can't stop. With tired eyes, Amar watches me thinking. He drifts in and out of sleep.

I'm fidgeting with a wrapper from a protein bar when the ship suddenly changes direction. Bright pain bursts in my shoulder as it thuds against the wall. In the cargo hold, the crates creak worryingly.

For a long minute I can't move. I'm forced against the hard metal. We're probably swinging around to come in for landing. But it should be gentle, not like getting out of Earth's pull. Right?

Amar's hands open and close on his knees as he stares at the floor. He's wedged in tight, like a little kid in a cupboard. Any minute now we should feel the rumble of the ground under our ship. But it doesn't come. There's only the quiet juddering of the ship's regular thrusters. The sensation of pressure drops, then increases.

We're both pushed harder into the metal rib. I'm stuffed against Amar by the pressure. The stack of crates we're hiding behind shifts closer toward us, leaving only a small gap.

We're accelerating? A lot! It's hard to breathe again. What's happening? Why have we changed direction? We should be landing.

"What's going on?" Amar says, too loudly. His voice bounces off the crates, and we both flinch.

There's a yell in the cargo hold. Someone shouts, "Go, go!"

Amar looks at me, terror-stricken. He's given us away! He cowers against the wall. He looks so small and young all of a sudden. I angle myself in front of him, as if I can protect him. I feel like I'm the adult. They'll have to start with me.

As I watch, holding my breath, two hands reach in toward us. Brown fingers wrap around the side of a crate. They're about to pull it away. Instead a face appears in the gap.

The person is spitting mad. But she's not mad at us. It's the captain I saw earlier. Her dark eyes meet mine. A larger hand appears behind her and grabs her by the hair. She's hauled backward, out of sight.

She yells, "Get off, argh, you starshit! I'll kill you! I'll kill you if you take my ship!" But she doesn't let on that she saw us.

"Good luck doing that from the void." The man who grabbed her has a hard, emotionless voice. There are sounds of a struggle, then an awful, meaty thump.

"Put her in the airlock with the others," the man says coldly. "As soon as we're fully clear of the shipping route, have Panda get to work on them. Anyone who doesn't cooperate can go out the dark door. We need to find out how to open these things without killing them." A slapping noise echoes through the cargo hold.

Ice crackles through my chest, settling around my heart. Whoever these people are, they're killers. And there's no doubt that if we're found, we'll join the crew in the airlock.

They're heading into dark space, away from the shipping routes. They must be pirates.

We're screwed.

"They's gonna kill them," Amar whispers, horrified.

Nausea swirls in my stomach. I think I might vomit. I'm no stranger to death—no one in the slums is. I've seen the crushed bodies of miners after collapses. The sick, the starving, the addicts. Fights that got out of hand. I've seen corpses. I've even seen a few people die, although I always tried to avoid it.

The terrified eyes of the captain are stuck in my head. I can still see the look in them. They're going to kill her, throw her out into space. She and Silly Man were laughing not long ago. Now they'll die. I wish I hadn't seen her face.

Sour saliva gathers under my tongue.

"We gotta *do* something," Amar says.

I have to take slow, measured breaths to keep from throwing up. "Do what? We're going to die too! Don't you get it? Those people will find us and throw us into space."

"That's why we gotta help *now*!" Amar's voice is getting louder. I flap my hand at him to make him shut up.

"You is *good*, Brick. I seen you give food to the littles. Even though you don't got extra. We can't just let them die. We gotta help them."

We, he says. As if we're some kind of team. My mind is racing. Amar is watching me like he expects a solution right away. He thinks I'm smart enough to snatch some wild idea from midair and save us. He thinks I'm kind just because I don't like watching children starve to death. I laugh as quietly as I can. It's not a good, happy laugh.

If we're seen, we'll be thrown out with the crew. We could stay hidden until the ship gets wherever it's going. But the pirates obviously aren't going to land anywhere we can stay. Probably some black-market moon somewhere, where they'll divide up their haul and sell it. Nowhere good. I search my brain, running through everything I can think of.

Amar's staring at me. His eyebrows are drawn down so tightly I can hardly see his eyes.

What is my idea? My thoughts slip and slide away from me. My pulse is hammering so loudly I'm surprised there's no echo. How are we going to survive this? I beg my brain for a plan. Just a whisper of an idea.

Chapter Eight

It hits me like an electric shock. The shuttles! This ship has two of them, which means one is on the same side as the airlock entrance. Someone could, in theory, steal a shuttle. They could try to line it up with the airlock and...catch the expelled crew. Then the crew would probably know what to do, how to get back onto a traffic route. How to make contact with someone who could save us if there isn't enough fuel.

It's a ridiculous idea.

It's the only one I have.

Amar's face clears, like he knows I've thought of something. There is a small, cold voice in my head. It's telling me it would be better to just stay hidden and hope we don't get caught. They'd throw us out into space, sure, which is the worst thing I can imagine. Except, perhaps, not living up to the hopeful look on Amar's face. The belief in his eyes that I'll get us out of this.

But I don't know how to fly a shuttle. I've played the arcade games, when the dust storms were so bad we couldn't be anywhere without air filters. Maybe that will help?

Starshit.

If I think about it any more I won't do it. I won't do anything. I can feel paralysis creeping up on me.

A deep sort of stuckness gluing me to the floor. I take a huge breath and force myself up.

My legs shake, mostly from terror, partly from being crouched in a ball for hours. I have to use the bathroom—badly. Maybe the pirates will let me hit it before they kill me. It would be less embarrassing that way.

I don't fall over, which I'm quite pleased about. Amar uncurls behind me. He stands, pressing himself against my back. It doesn't feel odd anymore. We've been crammed close together for so long it's become normal. I would have stayed leaning against him forever if he didn't push me forward. Solid, firm Amar. His iron belief in me, for some reason I don't know. He'd seen me feeding the littles, he said. Instead of seeing that as a weakness to be exploited, he saw it as strength. He sees me as strong.

Filling my lungs with the deepest breath I can, I move toward the gap.

We're toast if there's anyone left in the cargo area. My throat is so tight I can't swallow. My own muscles are choking me. The narrow space means I have to commit to leaving our nook. There's no way to poke my head out without the rest of my body. The heavy crates are fastened to the floor with long straps looped through metal rings. But some of the straps were broken earlier when the ship accelerated. If the weight shifts while I'm between the crates and the metal rib, I'll be crushed.

I don't breathe until I'm past the gap. I emerge between two huge stacks, easily double my height. From here I can see some of the cargo bay and more of the metal walkway that surrounds it. I hold myself as still as I can while I glance around. Movement would draw attention if anyone's watching, on cameras or otherwise.

Amar squeezes through the gap and waits. Nothing happens as I ease my way across the hold and to the stairs. Halfway up I can see most of the big room. No one's down here. I wonder how many pirates there are. Someone has to be flying the ship, and there were at least two people with the captain. I can't fight. My skills are limited to a few twisting escape moves. Amar's big and solid. He can be relied on. But even the best fighters have trouble when they're outnumbered.

A crowbar is stuffed into a cubby near the stairs. I beckon to Amar to join me, then jab my finger in the direction of the crowbar. He stops with one foot on the bottom stair, confused, and I mime bashing someone over the head. His mouth twitches and he nods. He grabs the crowbar and hands it to me.

We creep through the ship. Amar is a silent shadow, light on his feet but looming large. My fingers hurt where they're wrapped tight around the metal bar. I hold it like an old-timey batball player, over my shoulder, ready to swing. There's a pretty good chance that if we run into anyone, I'll shriek and run away. But I can pretend to be brave.

The hallways are spookily silent. We inch past a doorway marked with a toilet symbol, and my bladder spasms. I cringe. It would be stupid to stop, but I want to. Maybe I want to lock myself in the crew toilet and hope nobody notices.

I walk steadily past. We can't move too quickly—I have to listen. The sound of the engine had settled into the back of my head, but it's quiet now. My good hearing has saved me many times over. I'm on full alert for any sound, a whisper of cloth or the scuff of boots. But the faint buzz from the light strip is the only thing I hear.

Getting to a shuttle occupies my whole brain. There aren't many hallways to choose from. But we definitely don't want to go any farther up the ship. The next open doorway feels different, and I stop abruptly. There's something there! A faint whistle, like someone is breathing through a broken nose. My whole body tingles like an exposed nerve as I slide toward the doorway.

We have to go past. It's the only choice that isn't *up* toward the cockpit. The soft rags tied around my feet don't make a sound. I peer around the thick doorjamb. In the canteen a large woman with a gun instead of a forearm is struggling to open a jar. She can't get a grip on it. It would be funny but for the *gun for an arm* part of it. I dive past the doorway, reaching back for Amar's hand. He moves with me, fast and sure.

"Oi, you little shit."

The voice makes me freeze, but Amar bundles me onward, and we sprint flat out for the shuttle.

Behind us there's a clatter and then a satisfied sigh. Relief floods me in a hot rush. It wasn't us that made the pirate yell out! She must have been yelling at the jar. The hatch for the shuttle is in front of us. There's a large red handle. Amar grabs it before I can, heaving it downward. We stumble through the doorway and into the dark shuttle in a wild rush. We drop onto a hard surface, in a tangle of limbs.

The door slams closed behind us, sealing us into total blackness.

Chapter Nine

A heartbeat passes, two, and then the shuttle lights up. Rectangular panels and a cascade of buttons and screens illuminate the small space. The shuttle is around ten feet deep and eight feet wide. Storage-bench seating runs up each side until the cockpit. There are two pilot seats—one large and central, the other smaller and set back. Light bounces off the transparent aluminum window.

My stomach lurches and turns over. In front of me space rolls out, infinite and boundless. Sweat prickles all over my body, and ice washes through my veins.

"Would you like a vomit pouch?" a voice asks. We are still half lying on the floor.

In front of our sprawled bodies, a glowing blue head takes shape. A hologram. Vaguely humanoid, with minimal features.

"What?" says Amar, a little dazed.

"A vomit pouch." A drawer bursts open. I leap violently at the clanging sound. Inside there's a stack of white carbon-fiber baggies.

As it turns out, I would like a vomit pouch. I grab one and heave into it, acid burning my throat. I'm dizzy and off-balance, my whole self tilting. As if the vastness of space cancels out the artificial gravity.

A warm hand lands on my back, rubbing a soothing circle at the center. Amar. Unless this hologram has grown hands. I squint an eye open to check. Then close it again immediately.

"What the moon are you?" Amar asks. I can't see him, can't open my eyes, but he sounds scared.

"I am HARPOR. I am here to help," the hologram says.

I retch, miserable and useless.

"Why would you help us?" Amar sounds suspicious. "Are you with them pirates?"

"I am HARPOR—Holographic Auto-Responding Process Operational Resource. I am assigned to this mission. The mission captain is unable to respond. We detected malware designed to eliminate me in the main systems. When my captain realized we were under attack, she commanded that I move to this shuttle to broadcast MAYDAY. However, the pirates have installed a jammer, so I am at a limited capacity. Are you here to assist us?"

A shitty cargo ship like this should not have an AI assistant. It shouldn't have two shuttles either.

I remember the shiny white crates in the hold. I'd never seen anything like them before. Ten thousand queens, the captain said. I'm distracted enough that my stomach unclenches.

Amar tenses like he's going to say something, but I've finally managed to regain control over my mouth.

I yell, "Yes! Yes, we are here to assist you." My words come out mangled and raw, but I get my point across. Amar's fingers twitch on my back.

"Assigned: Acting mission captain. What are your orders?"

I carefully fold down the top of my vomit pouch to seal the waste. A drawer extends to receive it, and another slides out with a round water globule. It wibbles in my hands when I lift it out. I've seen them before, so I know what to do. The thin, elastic skin gives under my teeth when I bite it. Sweet water releases into my mouth, and I manage not to dribble it out. When it's empty, I pop the skin into my mouth and chew. *Ooh, minty.* Everyone is waiting for me to say something. I don't know how long it's been since HARPOR asked.

"Uh, can you fly the shuttle? We have to get to the airlock. Fast." With no idea how long we have until the crew is dead, speedier is better. The ship isn't moving anymore. That probably means someone's being tortured. Honestly, I don't really think there's anything we can do. We could just leave. This AI seems so friendly...maybe they will be easy to fool? I could tell them we have to go for help. But Amar is my friend, and he wants to help. I want to be a good friend.

"Assessing," HARPOR says. *"A pilot is necessary. I can perform navigation functions and act as copilot."*

"Can you tell me what to do?" I start toward the pilot seat, keeping my gaze unfocused. My whole body is straining for me to look out at the blackness.

But I know if I do, I'll puke again. If this AI is as smart as I want them to be, I will fly with my eyes closed.

"Negative. You are not suitable to pilot this vessel." HARPOR sounds almost apologetic.

Can HARPOR read my mind? "Look, pal, I'll figure it out, okay? I can handle it." I spit the words out from behind clenched teeth. Behind me, Amar shifts from foot to foot uneasily.

"You do not meet the height requirements for this vessel."

I stop, with my hand on the back of the seat. "You're kidding."

"A pilot must be five-point-five-feet tall in order to operate this vessel." There's a short pause. *"Your feet won't reach the pedals."*

Amar doesn't say anything, but he does come toward the main pilot seat. The hologram flickers and disappears. It was just at the back of the shuttle, where we dropped in through the hatch. Now it reappears above the controls set near the smaller pilot seat.

"We will need to open the rear compartment. You should put on a suit," HARPOR announces. A large cupboard pops open. Inside, two white sacks are hanging on a rack. Oh no. They're not white sacks. They're space suits. My mind replays *You should put on a suit.*

Everything goes soft and whooshy, and my knees stop working. My body folds down to the floor pretty gently. I black out like falling asleep between breaths.

"Acting Captain. Acting Captain."

I come around to the floating head of the AI that wants me to put on a space suit. I shut my eyes again, hoping it goes away.

"Captain, we are approaching the airlock. Our presence is masked to the ship's sensors. They do not appear to have noticed our detachment."

My eyes are squeezed firmly closed, but I've crawled over to the cupboard. My traitor hand feels around and grabs some fabric. It feels slick and silky, weirdly light.

"*Amar will also need a suit and a helmet,*" HARPOR tells me. "*It is vital you prepare before we depressurize the cabin.*"

I blink, not understanding.

"*Depressurize…*" HARPOR explains helpfully. "*To let all the air out.*"

Chapter Ten

I'm sure I'm green in the face, sticky with sweat and fear. There are no thoughts in my head, only a roaring sound. I could just pass out again. That sounds so relaxing. Maybe I'd even sleep through the attempted rescue. After all, the crew members we're trying to save don't have suits, do they? The memory of the captain being dragged away jumps back into my mind.

"How long can a human survive in space without a suit?" I ask. My voice sounds like it's coming from very far away. From someone else. I'm pulling on the space suit somehow. Standing up like my limbs won't take no for an answer.

"The maximum exposure for an average human male at peak fitness is approximately fifteen seconds."

"Helpful." How did I get to the back of the shuttle?

Amar is watching me from the cockpit. As long as I focus on his face, I don't have to look out the window. He's lit up by bright greens and blues from the dashboard. He has his face scrunched up again, eyebrows down. He *flew* here. He flew this space shuttle to the ship's airlock while I had a little panic nap on the floor.

My face rearranges, chin jutting, jaw tight. Eyebrows in and hard. Like Amar's. I square my shoulders. I drag Amar's kit to the front of the shuttle and pass it to him. I look only at his face, so I don't have to see what's behind him. Then I slam one of the helmets on over my head, determined. I'm doing my best impression of someone brave. Maybe if I pretend it, I'll believe it.

"That is backward, Acting Captain."

Once it's on the right way, the helmet seals itself to my suit with an odd crawling sensation. I shiver. It feels like bugs crawling on my skin. I'd rather this suit was full of bugs than deal with the fact that we're about to open this door. "Should I just clip myself on somewhere?" I ask HARPOR. I fiddle with the harness-like straps on my suit.

The AI is in two places now. One HARPOR is helping Amar with something at the front of the shuttle. I can't believe Amar flew us here. The HARPOR still with me cocks their head. *"You must use the main tether in order to reach the ship and release the door."* Their voice comes from inside my helmet, like they're in here with me.

I twitch my head, puzzled. "What?"

HARPOR extends a blue laser to point at a length of white rope rolled onto a large wheel. The whole thing is bolted down near the rear of the shuttle. *"Should we begin to depressurize, Acting Captain?"*

There's a high-pitched screaming inside my head. I'm a bit surprised it's not coming out of my mouth.

"Should we begin to depressurize, Acting Captain?" HARPOR repeats.

"You can do it, Brick. You can do anything!" Amar says, his voice inside my helmet too. He's fully suited up now. I can see his face through the large clear bubble of the helmet. The shapeless white sack now clings to his strong limbs. He looks confident and grown up. Confident in me, for some reason.

Steadying myself on the wall of the shuttle, I take the three steps toward the tether. My hands are shaking so hard. It takes a few tries to clasp the end of the tether to my suit.

"Ready to depressurize," I say, sitting down on the bench and making sure my tether won't tangle.

The false gravity in our shuttle slowly lets go of my body. I gently float off the bench, catching myself with one hand on the tether wheel and a toe braced against the wall.

I'm flying.

Somehow, in all my fears—of the dark, of the airlessness, of the sheer hugeness of space—I never wondered what it would feel like. To lose the weight of my body. The heaviness of myself.

I've always been a good climber, quick with my hands and feet. Able to run and jump and grab, to spring from place to place. I love the moment before gravity grabs me in its fist again. The sense of freedom, just for a moment. But this. Now. This is more than I ever could have expected.

Tears sting my eyes, and I've forgotten to be afraid. Forgotten to be breathless and panicked in the face of the universe. The door is open, and all I am is awed.

The larger shape of the main ship blocks most of my view. But between us—"below," if such a thing exists anymore—I can see forever. The infinity of space stretches and stretches on. This time I'm part of it. I'm part of everything.

I'm weeping as I let go of my handhold. Without gravity, tears become blobs and pool in my eyes. It feels horrible, but I don't care. My helmet siphons the liquid away. My body sways, lifts. My feet tumble over my head. I'm "upside down." I laugh out loud, looking for Amar in the pilot seat. I want to share this with him, but he's strapped in and serious, watching me through his bubble helmet.

The air inside my suit tastes faintly of something metallic. I'm not sure how any of it works, but there's no strain on my lungs or mind. The way to move feels familiar, as if my body already learned it on the streets. Flinging myself from buildings and trusting my hands and feet to catch me. As though a decade of doing that was all for this. A space walk. I wish I could see Earth from here. I bet it's beautiful.

My in-helmet display pops up with directions, and HARPOR controls my suit biometrics. I'm steered by small puffs of gas from valves on my suit. All I have to do is drift like fabric on a breeze. Float through nothingness to the hatch. I'm moving slowly enough that I flutter onto the side of the ship. There's an access path on either side of the hatch. It's made of loops and dents set into the surface of the ship. I settle myself near the hatch.

"Lift the lid and enter the code on the pad," HARPOR says. My helmet screen shows a bright-blue border around the access panel. Very handy. I scrabble at the lid for a moment, then get it open. The cover retreats into a slot in the ship, revealing a glass pane set with numbers. The code scrolls

across my screen, and I slowly copy it onto the keypad.

I can't read well, but this is basically a matching game. I manage to get the code in on the second try. The screen projects some words and two buttons, a red one and a green one. HARPOR makes the green one flash, and I push my thumb against it.

Something inside the ship rumbles, moves. Then there's a very faint hissing sound. Some numbers and data appear inside my helmet, which I'm sure would be very useful if I was actually a spacewalker. It's mostly just giving me a headache. I understand the vertical bar that's getting smaller and smaller, though. Inside the airlock the crew must be panicking, thinking they're about to die.

Well, there's a pretty decent chance they still might.

The keypad lights up again, and HARPOR guides me through the selections. I'm floating in nothing, typing in a code dictated by an AI. All to try and save multiple lives. It doesn't make any sense. But here I am.

Finally, with one last button tap, the airlock door begins to open.

Chapter Eleven

The airlock door swings in, away from me. It's so much bigger than the shuttle hatch. It's thick metal with multiple layers. As it opens, I can see the inside of the frame. It's full of complicated-looking bars and cogs.

HARPOR has started a countdown on my helmet screen. Fifteen seconds.

I launch myself into the airlock as soon as there's room to get through the gap.

The crew members are holding on to each other in a clump, like they want to die as a group. They're floating but wrapped together. I can't speak with them, and we only have seconds before they die. Twelve seconds.

I hurtle toward them. Eleven seconds. Silly Man is clutching what looks like three other people to his chest. He's back in his jumpsuit. I take all this in fast. Ten seconds. When I thump into them, a shudder rolls through the group. Nine seconds. I hook my strong fingers around Silly Man's back harness. I hope he can hold on to the others. Eight seconds. My other hand grabs whoever I can under his arm.

"Now!" I yell into my helmet. But HARPOR has already begun retracting my tether. Seven seconds.

The slack goes out of my line and heaves me backward. Six seconds. The group of us spins in the air as a whole, a shambles of arms and legs. We slap into a wall. Five seconds. The tether yanks us sideways, through the open door and into space.

We shoot into the shuttle. The momentum of the pull slaps me against a wall and empties my lungs. My suit seems to have taken some of the sting out of the impact, but I'm still crushed. All the air inside me has been pressed out by the thud of bodies into mine.

Two seconds.

The door seals, and a hissing noise fills the room. False gravity activates and gently pulls the pile of us onto the floor. There's an elbow digging into my stomach, and I still can't get a breath. HARPOR is flitting across the ceiling in a flurry of flashing lights. Can an AI be anxious?

Slowly we wriggle free of one another. They're moving. They're moving! That means they're alive. Whoa. My eyes prickle, and I swallow around the rock that's blocking my throat. I spacewalked, and I saved—I look around with more purpose—four people.

There's Silly Man and three others. My helmet releases, which I assume means it's safe for me to breathe. I pull it off, looking from face to face.

Their eyes are bloodshot and bruised-looking. All their faces seem swollen and off-color. The captain is looking around wildly, her eyes as big as moons. Silly Man is patting his body down, like he's checking for injuries and can't quite believe he's in one piece. The last two are clinging to each other still. They're pressed together in every way they can. They're half-laughing, half-crying into each other's mouths. Oh. I get a flash of tongue that makes me cringe and look away. Gross.

"Uh, welcome aboard," I say with an awkward wave.

"*Captain*." HARPOR becomes a floating face again. "*What are your orders?*"

"Let's get the quark out of here," I say, rubbing my hands over my face.

"*Captain Lakshmi, what are your orders?*" HARPOR clarifies, and a little laugh bursts out of my chest. Of course.

Embarrassed, I look away, catching Amar's eyes. He's hovering at the pilot seat, looking at me with something like awe on his face. I wish I could just liquefy and seep into the walls.

Captain Lakshmi gets to her feet and taps one of the couple on the shoulder. The two spring apart like they've been electrocuted. "HARPOR, report." Her voice sounds broken and cracked but determined. "Baines, Silvera—" She's cut off as the whole shuttle lurches. My feet go out from under me. As I fall, my arm hits the bench seat with a crack, and I cry out in pain.

"Captain, it appears the pirates have opened the airlock and learned of your escape."

Something hits the shuttle, and my stomach rolls as we're pushed into a spin. The gravity is no match for the force generated by the whirling ship. All I can do is cover my head with my arms and wait for it to stop.

Fortunately, at least one person has a better plan than yelling "oh shit, shit, shit" while bouncing off hard surfaces.

Someone's fired the engines, and the shuttle breaks free from the spinout. The floor is down again, and gravity and down are in the same direction.

I thud gracelessly to the ground, like I didn't spend most of my life falling off things on purpose. Luckily, my suit has protected me from any major major injuries.

Stiff and sore, every muscle protesting, I climb onto a bench seat. And strap myself in as fast as possible. Once I'm safely secured, I glance around.

Amar! He's sprawled out on the floor. His eyes are closed, and there's bright-red blood on his face. The captain is leaning over him.

My seat belt stops me from flinging myself toward him. "Amar!" I never knew my voice could get so high. "Amar! Is he okay? Help him!" I yell.

"I am," the captain says as she pats Amar down.

I can't swallow, can't blink. I did this. I brought him into space to die on some stupid hero mission. I'm not heroic. I should never have let him talk me into this.

Chapter Twelve

The captain's busy with Amar, and the kissing crew members are in the pilot seats. But Silly Man looks me over. He's on the bench opposite, carefully wrapping his wrist with a bandage.

"Stars, small fry. How old are you?" He sounds shocked.

Ugh, typical. I bet they think Amar's my dad or something. Gross. I'm not even really *trying* to look young right now. Although, when I do, I *do* usually go for scared and vulnerable. Which…yeah, I am both now.

"None of your business," I manage to say. I sound all wet and globby. "In case you didn't notice, we just saved you from a horrible death."

The man lets out one of those laughs that isn't really a laugh. "Sure as shit ain't safe yet…" He trails off, looking for my name.

"Brick." I swallow hard, trying to clear my throat. "That's Amar." I can't look over at him, in case he's dead. There's a cold, hard thing blocking my airway.

"Owasu. Captain Lakshmi"—he juts his chin toward her—"and Baines is the copilot, Silvera's the pilot. Just how did you come to be in the right space at the right time?"

I'm not sure how to answer that. The absolute nonsense that's happened to me today is endless. I'm never going to be normal again. I have *seen the universe.*

I curl up into a ball. At least, as best I can while strapped into a space shuttle. "Uh. Stowed away...ran away from the angry pirates. Met HARPOR." The AI is nowhere to be seen right now. "They got Amar to fly...and me to, well, open your hatch. So like...give us a head start before you report us?" I figure it'll come to that.

The shuttle rattles, metallic clangs ringing throughout. I flinch, looking around wildly for my helmet. We must've been hit, but no one else looks alarmed. In fact, Owasu is...unclipping himself? Oh. We're not moving anymore, and the engines are shutting down.

Oh no. We've reattached to the ship.

The ship full of pirates. Who know we're here. Who want to kill these people.

I can't make words happen—my mouth is moving without sound. I'm blank with fear.

The shuttle becomes a flurry of activity. My eyes dart around, taking in visual information without really processing anything. The pilots have left their seats. And are fitting themselves out with *weapons.* I see stun sticks. They've taken them out of a weapons locker.

Amar has been strapped to some kind of board. There's a thick band across his brow, holding his head in place. More straps wrap around his torso and hips. He looks almost gray-green instead of his usual terra-cotta. My heart is trying to break its way through my chest. Beating like a frightened rabbit's. My lungs don't work anymore. My vision starts to speckle, stars dancing in front of my eyes.

"Brick, hey!" Strong hands grasp my shoulders and stop me from slumping. "Frakking shit. Boss, the fishlet is sparking out." The words sound like they're coming from a long way away. I can barely make them out through the whine in my ears.

Fishlet! Ugh. That's even worse than "small fry." I try to complain, and my chest releases. Lovely air fills me up, tingles through my veins and clears my head.

"Is he dead?" I manage to say.

Owasu's large round face is sympathetic. He has kind eyes, dark as space and just as deep. I breathe with him.

"Nah, if he was dead they wouldn't need to hook him up." He points across the shuttle, and I focus. He's right! Amar's linked to some kind of monitor that's all lit up with flashing lines and numbers. Surely those mean he's still with me. The thought shocks me. Since my mom died, I've been basically alone. Sure, I know people and do favors. And I had to trade with people, or I'd have starved. But I haven't sat near anyone the way Amar and I sat shoulder to shoulder. I haven't laughed with someone or been comforted by someone in years.

Somehow, in less than a day, Amar has become my family.

The thought brings tears to my eyes, but they don't spill. I swipe them away with the backs of my hands. Amar is helpless. I have to protect him.

"I'm staying with him. Give me something to fight with." I sound stronger than I feel.

Owasu gives me an assessing look. Up and down, trying to figure me out. I channel Amar with everything I can. "Suppose I don't have a better idea what to do with you. Captain?" He turns toward the captain, who's busy with HARPOR, studying a floating picture of the main spaceship.

She looks up and nods for Owasu to speak.

"Brick here wants a weapon," he says.

The captain also looks me over, but quickly. And then she nods. "All right, give"—I make the "they/them" sign against my chest, and she nods again—"them a quick show-and-tell." She tosses something to me.

I do not catch it. Instead I flinch and fling my hands up to block my face. It doesn't hit me. When I peek around my palm, I see that Owasu has caught it. He rolls his eyes but gives me a quick tour of the weapon anyway. It's a shock stick. Basically an on/off, good-end, bad-end situation.

My hand is trembling so much it adds a little vibration action.

Captain Lakshmi strides over and wraps her hand around mine. It steadies my grip. Her palm is warm and dry. She gives me a wicked smile. "Fuck 'em up and save the world, Brick."

I don't care that much about the world. I just want to keep my friend safe. "What should I do if you don't come back?"

Her mouth pulls tight. "Get HARPOR to get you to the moon. Throw yourself on the mercy of the governors."

I don't tell her I'm too short to pilot. Maybe I can rig up a system somehow. The thought of landing a stolen shuttle on the moon is not appealing. "Please come back."

She gives me a grin. I don't think she intends it to be sexy, but it comes out that way. Something feral and hungry. "I usually do."

With that she's gone, following her crew members through the hatch. HARPOR closes the door, but not before I hear the start of violence breaking out.

I gulp and move closer to Amar, standing just in front of his prone body.

There's nowhere to hide in this whole shuttle. Not unless I fold myself up into a bench seat. I can't even stand behind the door because of the way it opens upward. My palms are sweaty and slippery. The stick threatens to slide out of my grip. My knees are shaking, and I try to pretend that it's from tension, from energy.

What are the chances the crew will get taken down? They did before. Sure, it was a surprise, I guess. But that woman I saw with the arm gun didn't look like she'd go down easy. I can't fly away unless Amar wakes up. All I can do is stand here and wait.

The hatch door hisses, making me jump. My teeth dig into the inside of my cheeks, where I'd sucked the flesh between my teeth. The taste of blood stings my mouth—metal and salt. The door swings open, up toward the ceiling. The woman stands framed in the entrance, lit by the eerie blue shuttle lights. Her arm gun is up and aimed right at me.

Chapter Thirteen

The pirate sneers, her face pulled into a horrible scowl. Her hair is dark brown and ear length, shaved away underneath. Muscles flex in her shoulder as she fires the gun.

My panic response is to fling my shock stick wildly in the direction of the threat. I watch, and it feels like slow motion. The shock stick loops lazily end over end, sparkless. It won't work if I'm not holding it—and I've *thrown* it away.

Two thick metal barbs dart through the air toward me. They spool out thin wires behind them. Not a gun, a taser! I guess firing bullets around inside a fragile metal shell isn't a good idea. The shock stick passes right through the taser barbs and snags them! It's caught the wires! Just inches away from my cringing body, the barbs are snapped back.

The electrified barbs loop through the air in a circle. Then they swing back under their own tension. Everything sparks. And then the bundle of shock stick and taser bits—the wires and the barbs—collide with the surprised pirate.

Her whole body seizes and shudders, jerking backward. She falls in the doorway, the shock stick on top of her. Her body spasms. Suns! The shock stick must be carrying the taser charge. Or the taser has turned the shock stick on somehow.

Electricity dances over the pirate's body like lightning. She continues to spasm. Her taser gun crackles and grinds. I'm too scared to touch her, in case the electricity jumps to me. I don't know enough about how any of it works!

A low groan grabs my attention. Amar! I drop to my knees with a dramatic clang.

"Amar? Amar!" I touch his face gently, his cheek and jaw. "Wake up, bro."

He makes a choking noise, trying to move. His eyes burst open, rolling in panic.

"Stay still! It's okay." I hold his head as carefully as I can, scared I'll make his injuries worse.

He calms a little, panting thickly through an open mouth. "Let me up. Let me up now, Brick." He doesn't sound calm.

"You have to stay still. You're hurt," I say.

"Let me up. I can't...I can't..." His voice goes thin and ragged.

I know the sound of panic. My hands fumble for the straps, pulled by the need in his voice. "Okay, okay. Calm down, and just stay as still as you can. I'm letting you out." I mumble nonsense as I unclip him. I could be letting him hurt himself worse.

Amar does as I say, lying still like a corpse. Except that every muscle in his body is flexed and shaking with tension. I saw a guy with his head dented in once. He was awake, kind of. But he couldn't move his body at all. So surely this is good, this movement— even if it is in fear.

Finally the last clip gives, and the tension flows out of him. He goes loose on the board, breathing deeply. "Thank you."

My hand is flat on his chest. I can feel his heartbeat slowing down under my palm. I want to ask him how he's feeling, but I also don't want to know.

HARPOR interrupts our silence. *"The pirates have been disabled. Amar, your vitals are good. The crew members ask that you join them in the cargo hold, if you're able to."*

The ship rumbles to life.

"What about her?" I jerk my chin at the pirate, who's still twitching in the doorway.

A panel pops open, displaying what appears to be a handgun. I recoil immediately.

HARPOR bobs into place next to me, shaking their head. *"It is only a tranquilizer. Once she is sedated, wrap your hand in the suit to push the shock stick free. She will remain unconscious for some time."*

I follow the instructions, then try to help Amar to his feet. Since he weighs about twice as much as I do, I'm not much use. I hover awkwardly, trying to support his elbow, but he takes most of his own weight.

We make our slow way down to the cargo hold. HARPOR beams out from various sensors to show us where to go, but I remember the route.

Getting down the stairs with Amar seems impossible, but Owasu sees us and thuds up the stairs. The man is an entire unit. He takes Amar's weight easily and helps him down the two flights. I've lost my rag shoes somewhere along the way. My bare feet scuff along the cold metal, so different from the dry dust and stone I'm used to.

In the hold, Captain Lakshmi is standing by the small white containers I noticed before. We join her, and Owasu sets Amar down so he can lean against a stack of crates.

The captain turns toward us, a broad grin on her face. There's a cut over her right eye, and she's holding her ribs. But she's so happy, I sort of smile back.

"I wanted to show you two what you saved today. I don't know what sent you to us, to this ship, but we needed your help. And you gave it to us." She's tearing up, which is awkward. I inspect the boxes with my eyes but can't see a way to open them.

Captain Lakshmi presses a few spots on the smooth surface, and the crate hisses. The front panel lifts away and scoots back into the box, exposing a clear screen.

I step closer, drawn in.

"Bees. Queen bees. Of the Cape variety. Each capable of reproducing independently." The captain pauses, her face going hard. "They were being sent to a station nearby to be used for facial cream. Cream! When Earth needs bees so things can grow. No wonder our planet is a wasteland, with rich people acting so selfishly and stupid! We found out and jacked the original crew. Clearly we weren't the only ones who had the idea to steal them. But we're taking them where they're needed. Back to Earth. To the people trying to fix things. The rebels."

I take another few steps, until I'm close enough to see inside the box properly. It's divided into segments, each filled with some kind of goo. Inside the goo, little white grubs wriggle. They look like fly maggots, the kind that eat rotten flesh and can be used to clean a wound. But they're *bees*! Baby bees!

I've never even seen a bee. After the great exodus, when the rich left Earth, there just weren't any. And these bees can make *more bees*?

"Why didn't you just fly the ship straight from the port to the rebels?" Even the word *rebels* lights a fire in my belly.

She claps me on the shoulder, and my knees buckle. "We'd have been shot down in moments. We're lucky the mercenary group that got the jump on us didn't expect you."

"Well, to be fair, you didn't expect us either," I say, pressing my nose up against the panel and trying to get a better look.

"I did." I can hear the grin in Amar's voice. "I always expect Brick to do the right thing."

Acknowledgments

As always, a heartfelt thanks to my delightful wife, Marie, without whom I would be a puddle of anxiety and self-doubt. Alix, thanks for answering my questions and thinking through scenes with me even when I am essentially just waving a wooden spoon at you and yelling about electrocution. Eternal gratitude to the Orca pod, my new editor, Doeun, and everyone in the team who works so hard to bring these vital books into the world.

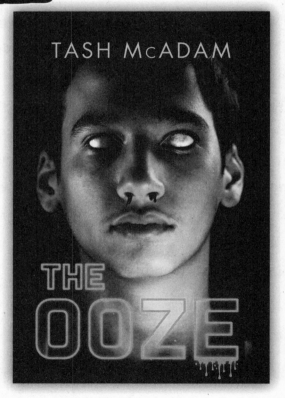

orca soundings

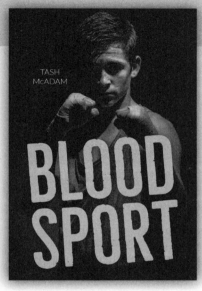

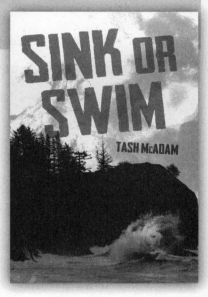

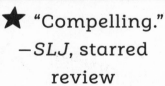

★ "Compelling."
—*SLJ*, starred review

"A gripping mystery."
—*Kirkus*

"A fast-paced and exciting perilous romance."
—*Kirkus*

Tash McAdam is a Welsh Canadian author, activist and educator whose books for young people include The Psionics series, the Junior Library Guild Gold Standard selections *Blood Sport* and *Sink or Swim* in the Orca Soundings line, and *The Ooze* in the Orca Anchor line. Tash is a recipient of the Shoot for the Moon fund for trans writers, and a founding mentor with the Gender Generations Project. They live in Vancouver, British Columbia.